The Ring Bearer

FLOYD
COOPER

PHILOMEL
BOOKS

PHILOMEL BOOKS

an imprint of Penguin Random House LLC
375 Hudson Street, New York, NY 10014

Library of Congress Cataloging-in-Publication Data
Names: Cooper, Floyd, author, illustrator.   Title: The ring bearer / Floyd Cooper.
Description: New York, NY : Philomel Books, [2017]   Summary: "Jackson's mom is getting married, and Jackson is nervous
about his role and his new family"—Provided by publisher.   Identifiers: LCCN 2015035947 | ISBN 9780399167409
Subjects: | CYAC: Stepfamilies—Fiction. | Weddings—Fiction.   Classification: LCC PZ7.C78485 Ri 2017 | DDC [E]—dc23
LC record available at http://lccn.loc.gov/2015035947   Manufactured in China by RR Donnelley Asia Printing Solutions Ltd.
ISBN 9780399167409
1 3 5 7 9 10 8 6 4 2
Edited by Jill Santopolo.   Design by Semadar Megged.   Text set in Paradigm.
Paintings were created using a subtractive process. The medium is mixed media.

For Niko

Mama is having a wedding,
and Jackson is worried.
What will it be like to call Bill "Dad"?
And share stuff with Sophie,
his new little sister?
Things won't be the same
around here anymore.

Jackson has an important job
at the wedding,
and he's not sure he can do it.

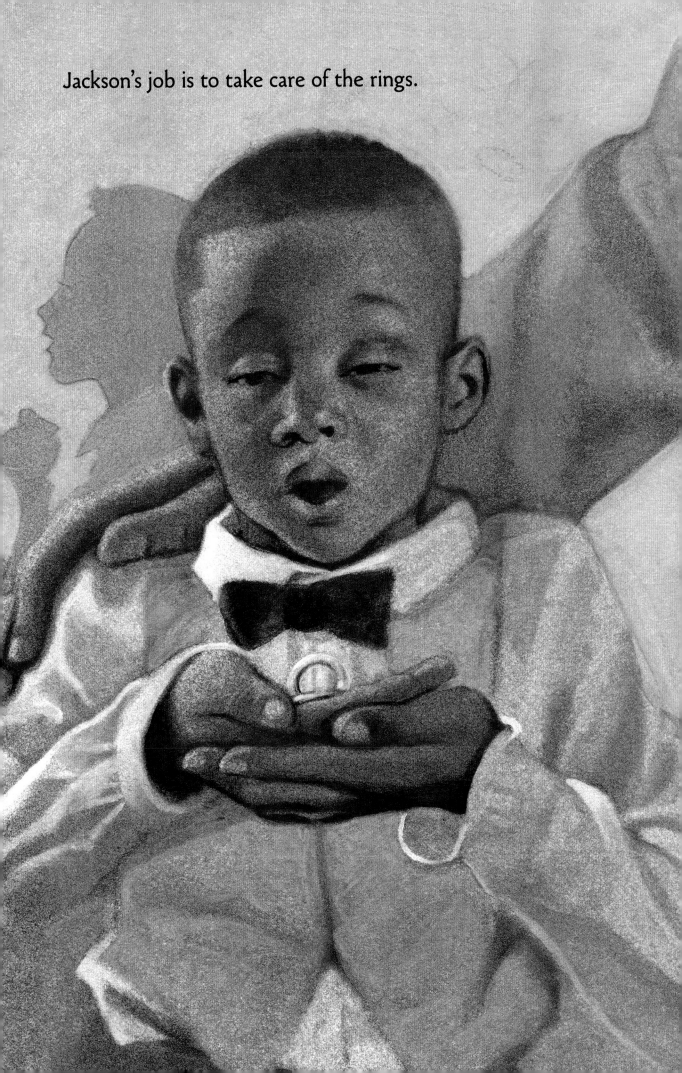

Jackson's job is to take care of the rings.

Bill walks by,
pinching his hanky at the middle.
He lifts it, flips it,
and folds it into his top pocket
to sit like a pet bird.
Jackson giggles, but he's still nervous.
Mama's having a wedding,
and Jackson has to carry the rings
down the aisle!

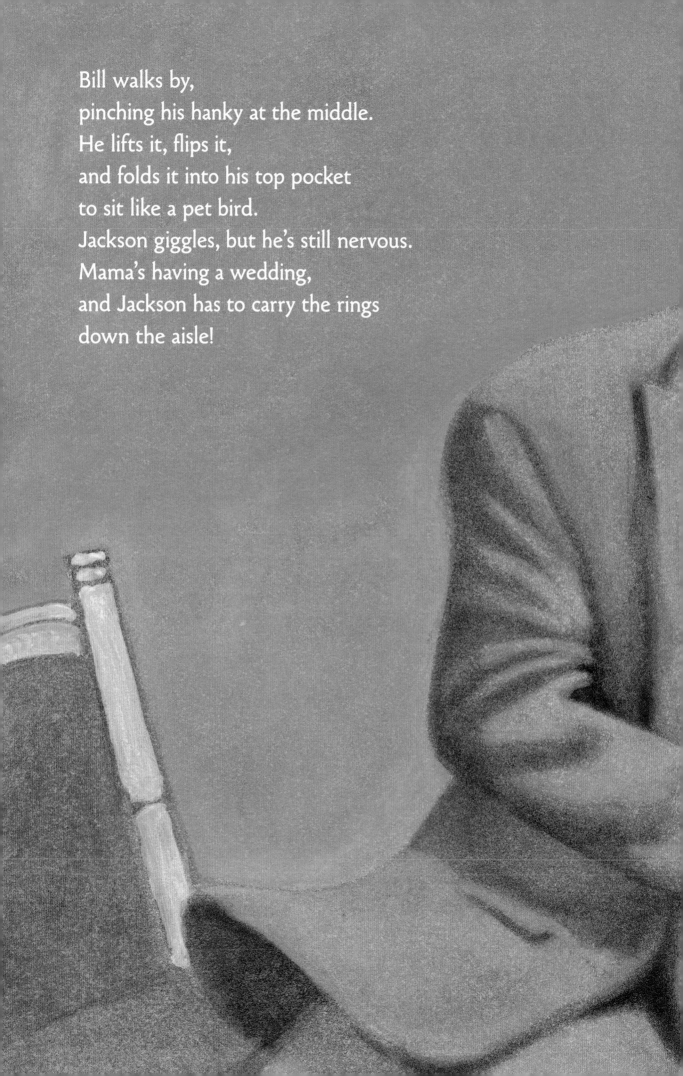

"Why the droopy shoulders?"
Bill asks as he lifts Jackson
high and makes him tall.

Jackson smiles on Bill's shoulders,
but inside he thinks, *Mama's having a wedding*
and I have to carry the rings,
but I don't want to trip in front of everyone
and mess it all up.
Maybe Bill should
carry the rings!

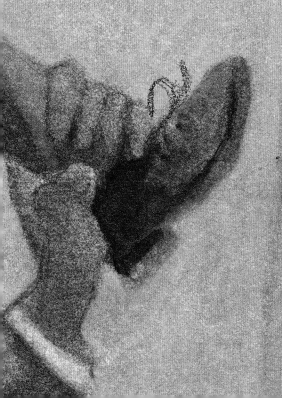

Tall Jackson walks over to little Sophie,
who is busy counting flowers.
Sophie has an important job, too—
she has to carry the flowers.

Grandpop helps them practice,
shows them how to walk down the aisle
slow and steady.
"That way, you won't trip,"
Grandpop says like he knows
just what's in Jackson's heart.

But Jackson is worried anyway.

The music starts and Sophie takes off.
Grandpop nudges Jackson
to get him going, too.
Jackson walks slow and steady
while Sophie skips ahead,
ignoring Grandpop's advice.

Mama's having a wedding,
and Jackson has
an important job to do,
and no matter what
Sophie does,
he will not trip down the aisle!

Jackson sees Sophie coming to a step,
but Sophie only sees her flowers.

Oh no!

Jackson rushes to Sophie
just as she trips on the step
and catches her before she falls.

Jackson looks at Grandpop.
Grandpop cheers.
Mama and Bill cheer, too.

The whole wedding cheers.
They're all cheering for Jackson!

Sophie smiles and grabs Jackson's hand.
They walk together,
slow and steady,
the rest of the way.

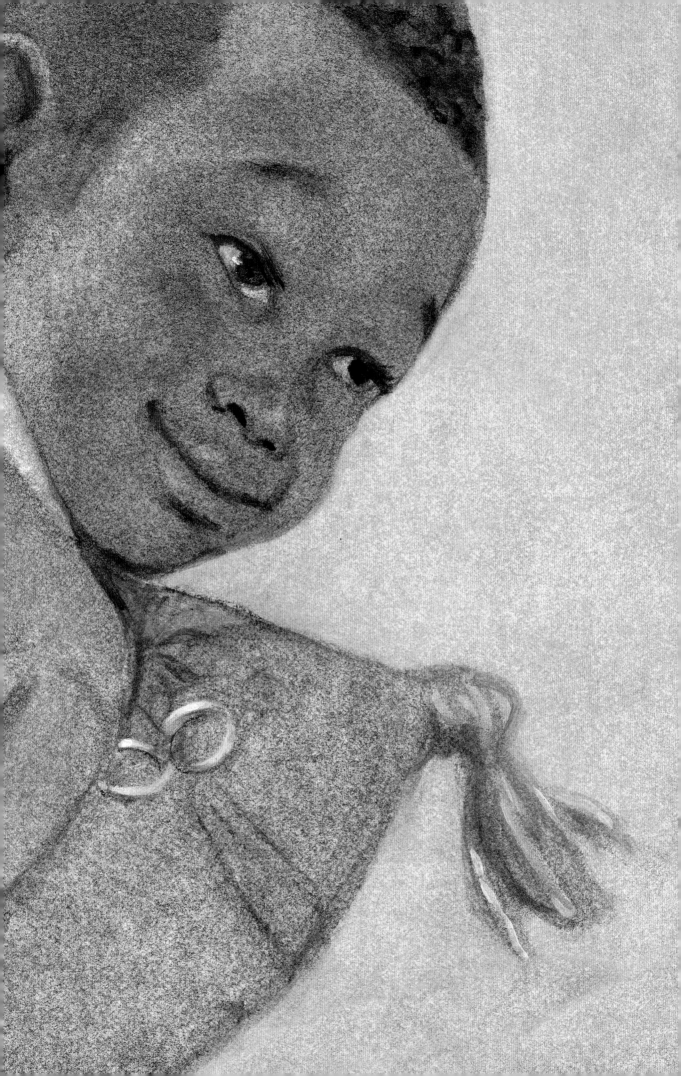

Sophie stands next to her dad.
Jackson waits for his mama,
who is coming down the aisle now
with Grandpop by her side,
looking like the prettiest lady
in the whole church.
Jackson sneaks a peek at Sophie,
making sure she is still okay.

When Mama gets to the end of the aisle,
she bends down next to Jackson.
"You're a great big brother, Jack,"
she whispers.
"Sophie is lucky to have you around."

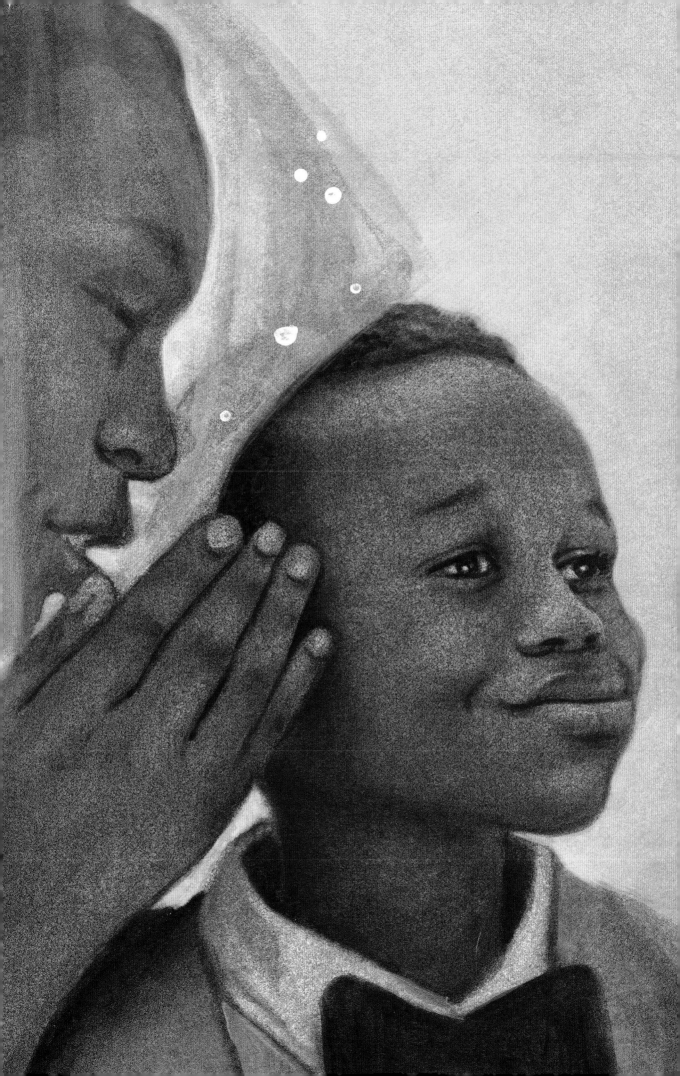

Looking at Mama and Sophie
and Bill and Grandpop,
Jackson is not worried anymore.
He's not nervous when he reaches
into his pocket for the rings.
He's not nervous when he gives them
to Mama and Bill.

And when the preacher finally says,
"They're all a family now,"
Jackson knows deep in his heart
that he doesn't have to be
so nervous about important jobs.
And he definitely
doesn't have to be nervous
about being a big brother.

Mama got married,
and Jackson handled his job
just right!